MR. MEN   **LITTLE MISS**

MR. MEN™ LITTLE MISS™ © THOIP (a SANRIO company)

Little Miss Busy Surviving Motherhood © 2017 THOIP (a SANRIO company)
Printed and published under license from Penguin Random House LLC
Published in Great Britain by Farshore

An imprint of HarperCollins*Publishers*
1 London Bridge Street, London SE1 9GF
www.farshore.co.uk

HarperCollins*Publishers*
1st Floor, Watermarque Building, Ringsend Road
Dublin 4, Ireland

ISBN 978 1 4052 8871 2
Printed in Italy
010

Stay safe online. Farshore is not responsible for content hosted by third parties.
Farshore takes its responsibility to the planet and its inhabitants very seriously.
We aim to use papers from well-managed forests run by responsible suppliers.

LITTLE MISS BUSY
SURVIVING
MOTHERHOOD

Roger Hargreaves

Original concept and illustrations by
Roger Hargreaves

Written by
Sarah Daykin, Lizzie Daykin and Liz Bankes

Little Miss Busy hadn't always been so busy. She used to enjoy lie-ins, lazy Sundays and leisurely all-night raves.

But then she had kids.

Now Little Miss Busy endures 5am wake-up calls, manic Mondays, Tuesdays, Wednesdays, Thursdays, Fridays, Saturdays and Sundays, and watching enough children's TV to send her stark raving mad.

It was another busy day and Little Miss Busy did what she did every morning: mainlined six cups of coffee and started writing her to-do list.

1. Write list
2. Make nutritious breakfast
3. Make kids eat nutritious breakfast
4. Swap nutritious breakfast for Choccy Yummy Pops
5. Tell kids to feed guinea pig
6. Tell kids to finish homework
7. Wake up husband
8. Tell kids guinea pig will die if not fed
9. Shake husband until he wakes up
10. Finish kids' homework
11. Feed nutritious breakfast to guinea pig

Little Miss Busy ticked everything off her list, and herded the children out of the door. She felt very pleased. 'Mum! I have to dress up as a Tudor tomorrow,' said the youngest child.

12. Make Tudor costume

Little Miss Busy arrived at the school gates. All of the other mums were there, and so was Mr Good, who they all praised for doing the school run. 'He's such a good dad!' they said. 'Look at him caring for his own children!'

Little Miss Sunshine's 4x4 pulled up. Her twins climbed out and skipped over to Little Miss Busy.

'We are learning Chinese!' they chimed in perfect unison. 'So we can get ahead in the world of business.'

'Wow!' said Little Miss Busy. 'How old are you?'

'四' they said.

Little Miss Busy looked at her own children who were fighting over a stick.

Little Miss Sunshine jogged over in her designer gym gear. 'Phew, what a morning! Pre-school pilates can really take it out of you,' she said looking fresh as a daisy. 'Have you made a cake for the school bake-off yet? I can't decide between macarons or a gingerbread Taj Mahal.'

'Yes, nearly finished!' said Little Miss Busy. She added 'Bake a cake' to her list.

'Anyway, must dash,' said Little Miss Sunshine. 'I'm making courgetti hoops for the kids.'

After going to the shops, picking up organic courgettes, and putting them back to buy fish fingers instead, Little Miss Busy went to see Little Miss Tidy to borrow a cake tin.

Little Miss Tidy was very neat and organised. She never got stray Lego bricks embedded in her foot, she never let the washing pile engulf the room, and she certainly never forgot World Book Day and sent the kids in wearing bin bag cloaks with scars scribbled in biro on their foreheads.

'I've got just the tin for you!' beamed Little Miss Tidy.

'Great! I'll get it,' offered Little Miss Busy.

'NO I HAVE A SYSTEM!' shouted Little Miss Tidy, heading for the kitchen. 'Oh and could you host book club tonight? As head of the PTA, I've got to alphabetise the cuddly toys for the raffle.'

'Of course!' said Little Miss Busy. She added 'Read *War and Peace* and make nibbles for eight' to her list.

Little Miss Busy got home, collected up all her recipe books and advice manuals and tried to ignore the 267 work emails, the bright red crayon on the wall and her growing suspicion that one of the children had weed in the plant pot.

How Not To Be A Terrible Mother
Baking Made Difficult
Dummies for Dummies
Tudor Costumes for the Whole Family

She was just trying to make a codpiece out of a toilet roll when the phone rang. It was her mother-in-law. 'I'm just in the area and thought I'd drop by unannounced!' her mother-in-law announced. 'Wonderful!' said Little Miss Busy.

She pulled out her copy of ***How Not to Murder Your Mother-in-Law***.

With a list now as long as Mr Tickle's arm, Little Miss Busy picked the kids up from school and sat them in front of the TV with some biscuits while she attempted to clean the whole house.

She had just enough time to cram the plastic toys in the airing cupboard, hide the PlayStation and tell the kids not to mention Granny's beard, before her mother-in-law, Little Miss Splendid, arrived.

'Don't get up!' she said. 'I'll make my own tea. Where is the china? You don't have china! No, no, don't worry. I shall have to survive with this mug.'

'Now, come and give your granny a kiss and tell me what you've been doing at school,' said Little Miss Splendid.

'I got a gold star!' said the oldest child.
'I got headlice!' said the middle child.
'Why do you have a beard?' said the youngest child.

After checking that the kids were on-course for Oxbridge, making sure that Little Miss Busy knew how to wash and iron Mr Busy's pants just how he liked and commenting that she looked 'as tired as a corpse,' her mother-in-law went on her way.

Little Miss Busy gave the kids their tea and then tucked into her own serving of half-chewed fish fingers and beans.

Now to make her prizewinning bake-off entry. She picked the first recipe she found: three-tiered meringue with a gooseberry mist. She was fresh out of gooseberry mist, so she sprayed it with air freshener and hoped no one would notice.

The kids helped, until she said they'd be much more helpful if they played in the other room, where they resumed fighting over a stick.

She settled down to read *War and Peace*. 'A thousand pages!' Wikipedia it was.

Then all of a sudden, she heard an almighty crash!

'MUM!' went the children. SPLAT! went the cake. THUD! went the codpiece.

'#~?&!!%#$!!!' went Little Miss Busy, as she fell onto the bed.

Little Miss Busy's phone rang again.

'No you can't pop round!!' she screamed.

But it wasn't her mother-in-law. It was her best friend.

'Sorry, I know I said I'd call you last week,' said Little Miss Late. 'How are you?'

It all came flooding out. And Little Miss Late listened. And gave her some very good advice.

'Get the cake from the supermarket. Tell them book club is off. And let your mother-in-law know that anyone who irons their pants is a psychopath.'

Mr Busy arrived home and was handed the kids, just in time for the nightly pyjama battle, and Little Miss Busy went to buy a cake.

But on her way she saw something very surprising indeed.

'One special fried rice, one sweet and sour pork balls . . .' said Little Miss Sunshine as she pulled up to the drive-thru takeaway.

'四! 四!' said the twins from the back seat.

'Yes, yes! And a number 4 – chow mein,' added Little Miss Sunshine.

Then she saw Little Miss Busy.

'They were out of courgettes!' she said desperately.

Little Miss Busy went to Little Miss Tidy's house to return the unused cake tin and tell her she couldn't host book club.

And Little Miss Busy saw something even more surprising.

'Wait! Don't come in!' said Little Miss Tidy.

Little Miss Tidy was buried under a huge pile of mess.

'I just make the front room look nice and then shove everything in here!' she wailed.

Little Miss Busy knew just what to do.

Book club was back on, but with less books and more bubbly.

'I've never actually done any exercise – I just wear the clothes to make it look like I do!' said Little Miss Sunshine. 'And when I say I'm doing pilates, I'm actually sitting in my car and eating cheese.'

'Last week I left one of the kids at the motorway services and had to bribe him with sweets not to tell anyone,' said Little Miss Tidy.

'I've fallen asleep in all of my daughter's recorder concerts,' said Little Miss Busy.

The revelations kept coming, and they all agreed that it's okay to serve fish fingers, wear pyjamas under your clothes and to eat all of the kids' Easter eggs and blame it on their dad.

All of the Little Misses stayed up laughing and doing karaoke with a broom.

The next day, Little Miss Busy's wake-up call arrived painfully early.

'MUUUUUUUM!'

Little Miss Busy played dead.

'MUUUUUUUUUUUUUUM!'

It was no use - she would have to get up and make a new list for another busy day.

'MUUUUUUUUUUUUUUUUUUUUMM . . .'

'. . . we've made you breakfast!'

And even though it was inedible, it was the best breakfast she'd ever had.

'Don't worry Mum, we'll do all of the jobs today!' said the kids.

And do you know what? They did!

Except one.

'Mum! The guinea pig's dead.'